Goodbye, Mousie

by Robie H. Harris
illustrated by Jan Ormerod

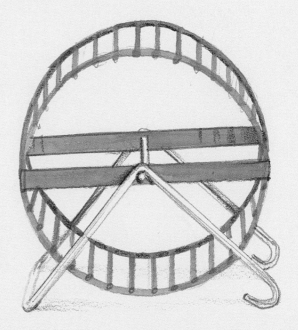

Simon & Schuster, London

When I woke up this morning, I tickled Mousie's tummy. But Mousie didn't wake up. I tickled Mousie's chin, but he still didn't wake up. Then Daddy came to say good morning.

"Mousie won't wake up!" I whispered. "I think something's wrong!"

Daddy took a good look at Mousie. Then he put his arm around me.

"I have something very sad to tell you," he said. "Mousie is . . . dead."

And then Daddy gave me a big hug.

"It's NOT true!" I said. "Mousie's just sleeping. He'll wake up soon. He's just tired. You're wrong! Mousie has NOT died! Mousie is NOT dead!"

Daddy sat down on my bed and I put Mousie in his hand.

"I'm so sorry about Mousie," he said.

"Mousie is NOT dead!" I said again. "Mousie was alive last night! He's just . . . very . . . very sleepy this morning."

"Dead," said Daddy, "is very different from sleeping. Dead is —"

"— NOT alive!" I shouted. And I started to cry.

"You must be sad," said Daddy.

"I'm not sad. I'm cross! I'm cross with Mousie. I'm cross he died!"

And then I cried. I really cried.

Then I said, "I'm sad."

"I'm sad too," said Daddy. And he gave me another hug.

"I want to hold Mousie again," I said. "I want to hold Mousie now."

"OK," said Daddy.

I held Mousie again, but he felt cold. So I wrapped an old T-shirt around him.

"I don't like Mousie dead!" I said. "Why did he die?"

"I don't think Mousie got hurt," said Daddy.
"But maybe he got too sick."

"Is that why he died?" I asked.

"Well," said Daddy, "Mousie was a baby when
we got him. He grew up. Then he grew old.
Mousie was very, very old for a mouse."

"So is that why he died?" I asked.

"I don't know if we'll ever know exactly why
Mousie died," said Daddy. "But Mousie did
have a good life."

"What shall we do with him now that he's . . . dead?" I asked.

"We can bury him in the garden so he'll be close by," said Daddy.

"But how will I know exactly where he is?"

"We could make a sign."

"Can it say, MOUSIE IS RIGHT HERE?"

"Sure!" said Daddy. And he wrote MOUSIE IS RIGHT HERE in big letters on an old wooden board we'd found at the beach.

I carried Mousie into the kitchen. Mummy gave me a hug and a kiss.

Then she gave me an extra hug and a kiss.

"I'm so sorry Mousie died," she said. And she handed me a shoebox.

"We could bury Mousie in this," she said. "Mousie will be safe in this."

I laid Mousie in the shoebox and tucked my old T-shirt all around him. Mummy made toast with strawberry jam on it for me. But I wasn't hungry at all.

"Do you think it's OK to bury Mousie with some toast?" I asked. "I always used to feed Mousie bites of my toast. Mousie loved toast."

"I think that would be just fine," said Mummy.

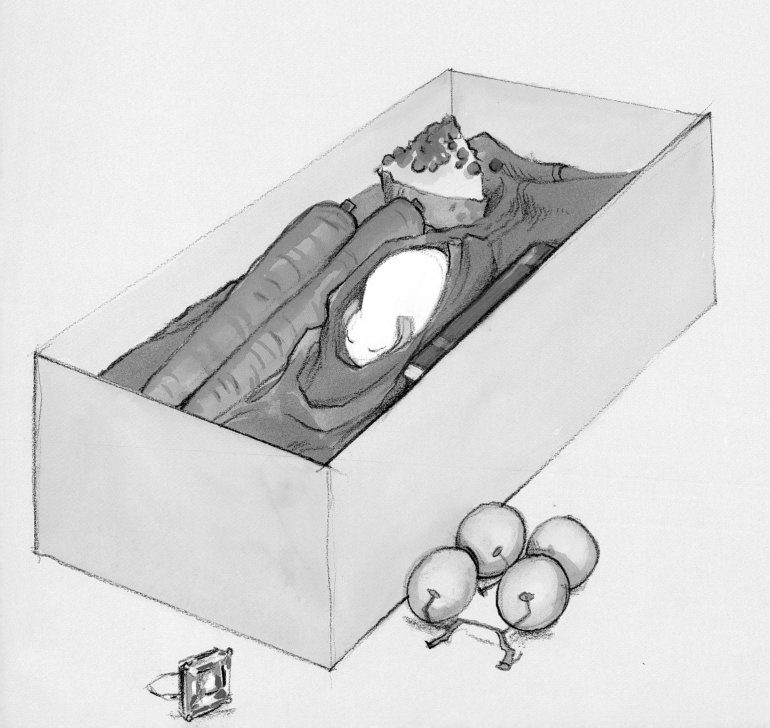

"Can I put more things in the box?" I asked.

"Of course you can!" she said.

I put some toast and two whole carrots on one side of Mousie. I put four grapes and a bar of chocolate on the other side.

"Now Mousie won't be hungry!" I said.

I put my red racing car in the box. I put a ring with a big blue jewel my dentist gave me in the box. I put an orange crayon in too.

"Now Mousie won't be bored!" I said.

I taped a picture of me in sunglasses to the inside of the shoebox.

"Now Mousie won't be lonely," I said.

Then I taped the box shut and looked at it. "Mousie's box looks too plain," I said. "And Mousie won't like that."

So I painted wiggly stripes all over Mousie's box. I felt a little bit better. And Mousie's box didn't look plain any more.

"It looks nice," said Daddy.

I thought it looked nice too.

I washed almost all the paint off my hands. And now
I was hungry. So I went to take a bite of my toast.
But it was all gone!

"My toast!" I shouted. "Where did it go? Has it died,
too?"

"Oh no, sweetheart!" said Mummy. "I ate it. I thought
you weren't hungry. I'm really sorry. I'll toast another
piece for you."

"I don't want one. And I hate all this dying!"
I cried. "Let's bury Mousie NOW!"

So we did.

Mummy dug a hole in the ground and I put the shoebox in the hole.

Daddy stuck the sign in the ground and I covered up the box with the soil.

Mummy lit two sparklers and I stuck them in the soil. We all watched the sparklers burn out. And I cried.

And then I said, "Mousie, I'm cross with you for being dead. I'm sad too. You were a good mouse. I'll miss you, Mousie."

Then I cried some more and said, "Goodbye, Mousie." That's all I said.

When I wake up tomorrow morning, Mousie won't be here. It's true. Mousie is dead.

I wish he would come back. But I don't think he will.
So, maybe someday, I'll get another mouse. But not just yet.